PHONICS

Splish, Splash!

Written by

Clare De Marco

Illustrated by

Gustavo Mazali

Practising CVCC and
CCVC plus polysyllabic words

First published in 2010 by
Franklin Watts
338 Euston Road
London NW1 3BH

Franklin Watts Australia
Hachette Children's Books
Level 17/207 Kent Street
Sydney NSW 2000

Text © Clare De Marco 2010
Illustration © Gustavo Mazali 2010

A CIP catalogue record for this book
is available from the British Library.

ISBN: 978 0 7496 9165 3 (hbk)
ISBN: 978 0 7496 9174 5 (pbk)

Series Editor: Jackie Hamley
Series Advisors: Dr Barrie Wade,
 Dr Hilary Minns
Series Designer: Jonathan Hair

Printed in China

Franklin Watts is a division of
Hachette Children's Books,
an Hachette UK company
www.hachette.co.uk

There is a puzzle at the end of this book.
Here are the answers for you to check later!

The matching words are:

splash crash, flash, trash

junk clunk, skunk, trunk

brush crush, flush, slush

skip drip, flip, strip

Jess and Tam were twins.

They were helping
Mum and Dad.

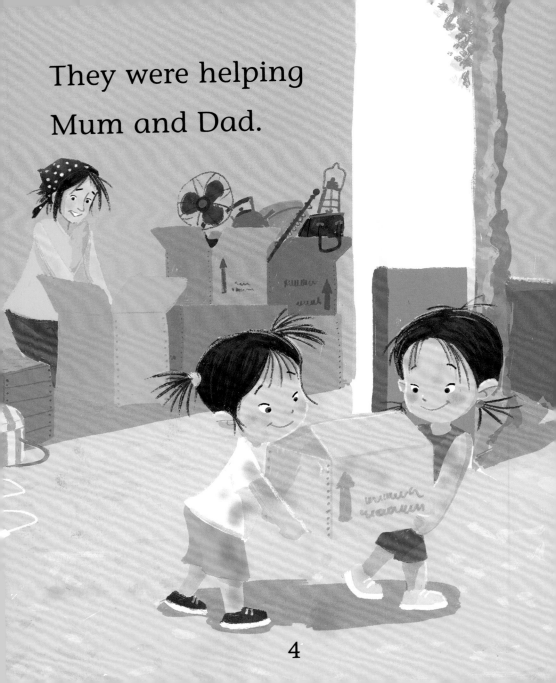

They all had to put lots
of junk in a skip.

6

"This stuff smells!" said Dad,
as a big box went crashing in.

"Yes," said Mum. "You children must get in the bath."

11

"I want to splish!" said Jess.

"And I want to splash!" said Tam.

"You can splish and splash!" said Dad.

"But not for long!"
said Mum. "You must
go to bed!"

15

Jess and Tam got in the bath.

Jess had a splish ...

... and Tam had a splash.

Jess had a splash ...

... and Tam had a splish.

Mum and Dad had a shock!

"Stop splishing and splashing ...

... and get dressing and brushing!" they said.

"And when we stop
dripping, we can go
to bed!" said the twins.

Puzzle Time!

Match the words that rhyme
to the pictures.

splash

flash

skunk

crush

flush

junk

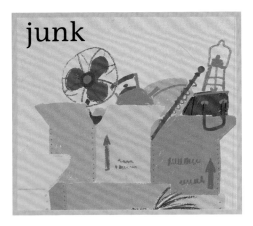

flip

trash

brush

trunk

strip

drip

clunk

skip

crash

slush

See page 2 for answers.

Notes for parents and teachers

READING CORNER PHONICS has been structured to provide maximum support for children learning to read through synthetic phonics. The stories are designed for independent reading but may also be used by adults for sharing with young children.

The teaching of early reading through synthetic phonics focuses on the 44 sounds in the English language, and how these sounds correspond to their written form in the 26 letters of the alphabet. Carefully controlled vocabulary makes these books accessible for children at different stages of phonics teaching, progressing from simple CVC (consonant-vowel-consonant) words such as "top" (t-o-p) to trisyllabic words such as "messenger" (mess-en-ger). READING CORNER PHONICS allows children to read words in context, and also provides visual clues and repetition to further support their reading. These books will help develop the all important confidence in the new reader, and encourage a love of reading that will last a lifetime!

If you are reading this book with a child, here are a few tips:

1. Talk about the story before you start reading. Look at the cover and the title. What might the story be about? Why might the child like it?

2. Encourage the child to reread the story, and to retell the story in their own words, using the illustrations to remind them what has happened.

3. Discuss the story and see if the child can relate it to their own experience, or perhaps compare it to another story they know.

4. Give praise! Small mistakes need not always be corrected. If a child is stuck on a word, ask them to try and sound it out and then blend it together again, or model this yourself. For example "wish" w-i-sh "wish".

READING CORNER PHONICS covers two grades of synthetic phonics teaching, with three levels at each grade. Each level has a certain number of words per story, indicated by the number of bars on the spine of the book:

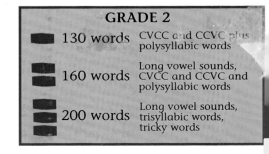

GRADE 1	
50 words	CVC words with short vowel sounds
70 words	CVC words plus sounds of more than one letter
100 words	Sounds of more than one letter, simple polysyllabic words

GRADE 2	
130 words	CVCC and CCVC plus polysyllabic words
160 words	Long vowel sounds, CVCC and CCVC and polysyllabic words
200 words	Long vowel sounds, trisyllabic words, tricky words